Quentin Blake

ZAGAZOO

A Tom Maschler Book
JONATHAN CAPE
London

for Tom

First Published 1998

1 3 5 7 9 10 8 6 4 2

© Quentin Blake 1998

Quentin Blake has asserted his right under
ther Copyright, Designs and Patents Act 1988 to
be identified as the author of this work

First published in the United Kingdom in 1998 by
Jonathan Cape, Random House, 20 Vauxhall Bridge Road,
London SW1V 2SA

Random House UK Reg. No. 954009

A CIP catalogue record for this book is available
from the British Library

ISBN 0 224 04723 X

Printed in Singapore

Once upon a time there was a happy couple.
Their names were George and Bella.

They spent their days…

…making model aeroplanes…

…dusting…

...and eating strawberry
and vanilla ice-cream.

One day the postman brought
them a strange-looking parcel.

They unwrapped it together.

Inside there was a little pink creature, as pretty as could be. On it was a label which said:

Its name is Zagazoo.

How lovely it was. George and Bella
spent happy days throwing it from
one to another.

Zagazoo was not *quite* perfect.

But his happy smile
seemed to make
up for that…

…and George and Bella went
on happily throwing him to each other,
higher and higher.
It was a wonderful life.

AND THEN ONE DAY…

…George and Bella got up in the
morning and discovered that Zagazoo
had changed into a huge baby vulture.

Its screeches were terrifying.

They were even worse at night.

"What shall we do?" said George.
"How can we stand it?"

But then...

…they got up one morning and discovered that Zagazoo had changed into a small elephant.

He knocked over the furniture.

He pulled the tablecloth off the table.

He ate anything he could lay his trunk on.

"This is appalling," said Bella.
"How can we cope?"

But then...

… one morning they got up
and discovered that Zagazoo had
changed into a warthog.

He rolled about in anything that looked
like mud and ran about the house with it.
"This is dreadful," said George.
"There's just no end to it."

But then...

…they got up one morning and discovered that Zagazoo had changed into a small bad-tempered dragon.

He scorched the carpet.

He set light to the cardigan of an old lady who had come to sell raffle-tickets.

"This is terrible," said Bella. "In no time he's going to burn the house down."

But then...

…they got up one morning
and discovered that Zagazoo had
changed into a bat that hung
on to the curtains and wailed.

And then the next day he was the
warthog again.

And then some days he was the elephant...

...and some days he was the bad-tempered dragon.

"This is driving us to distraction," said Bella. "If only he'd stay as one thing."

But then...

…one morning they got up and Zagazoo
had changed into a strange hairy creature.

"Oh no!" said Bella. "I preferred the elephant."
"Or even the warthog," said George.

Every day the creature went on getting bigger … and hairier … and stranger.

"Suppose it never stops," said Bella.

"It doesn't bear thinking about," said George.
"It's turning my hair grey already.

What will become of us?"

BUT THEN...

… one morning George and Bella got up
and discovered that Zagazoo had changed
into a young man with perfect manners.

"Let me get you a chair, Mama," he said.

"And let me get you both some breakfast."

"And if there are any odd jobs that need doing, just let me know."

Zagazoo soon made friends with a young
woman called Mirabelle.

They found they were both interested
in motorcycle maintenance ...

...flower arrangement...

...and eating fruit salad.

It was not long before
they knew that they wanted
to spend the rest of
their lives together.

But when they went to tell George
and Bella, they discovered that they had
changed into a pair of large brown pelicans.

You could tell they were pleased at the news
by the way they clattered their beaks.

Isn't life amazing!